# JUSTIN
# AND THE BEST BISCUITS
# IN THE WORLD

MILDRED PITTS WALTER

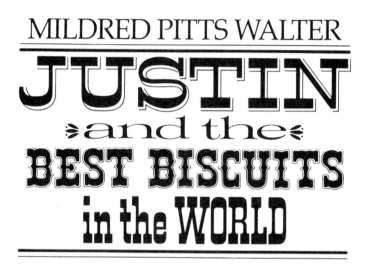

# JUSTIN
## ❧and the❧
# BEST BISCUITS
## in the WORLD

with illustrations by
CATHERINE STOCK

HOUGHTON MIFFLIN COMPANY

BOSTON

Atlanta   Dallas   Geneva, Illinois

Palo Alto   Princeton   Toronto

This book is dedicated to
Franklin Folsom and Paul Stewart
who have done much to preserve and gain respect
for true Western history and Western lore.

✺

Chapter 8, THE EXODUSTERS, is based on information
from the scholarly work, *EXODUSTERS: Black Migration to
Kansas after Reconstruction* by Nell Irvin Painter, first pub-
lished in 1977 by Alfred A. Knopf.

1995 Impression
Houghton Mifflin Edition, 1993

Printed in the U.S.A.

ISBN 0-395-61802-9

456789-B-96 95 94

# CONTENTS

# ♫ 1 ♫

## JUSTIN IS GROUNDED

THE BALL HIT the board and rolled around the rim of the basket. Justin reached his tallest, caught it on the rebound, and tipped it in.

"My win," Justin said to his friend Anthony. Surprised and pleased he had at last won, Justin said, "Let's play another game."

"I gotta get home, but tomorrow, OK?"

"Let's come early."

"I'll pick you up," Anthony said.

Justin still wanted to play one-on-one,

[1]

his favorite basketball game, but there was no one left to challenge him. The playground was emptying fast. Only a few girls were scattered about. Some played jump rope. Others played tetherball.

He watched the rope jumpers and had an urge to get into their game. His sudden, untimed move broke the rhythm. One girl threw down the rope and chased Justin, shouting, "You better stay out of our game!"

Justin ran fast, laughing at her. The girl soon gave up and went back to turn the rope for her friends. Justin returned to the basketball court. He zigzagged, dribbling the ball. Then he tried making long shots and missed them all. At the free-throw line he tossed twice and missed. Disgusted, he dribbled around the court again.

The August sun moved far westward. Rolling hills in the distance cast shadowy shades of purple. The playground was now quiet, deserted. Justin tossed for the basket. He hit. He tossed two more perfect shots and decided it was time to leave.

He walked along the tree-lined streets between rows of sturdy wood frame houses, wishing he didn't have to go home. Not yet. If only he had brothers; one brother, anyway. Somebody to help him control Evelyn, his older sister.

He turned the corner onto his block. Their car was in the driveway. His mother was already home. He hadn't known it was *that* late. Hadiya, his younger sister, strained under bags of groceries as she removed them from the car. That was his job. The one thing he did well enough around the house to win praise and approval. He needed to be home. He started running.

There was much talk, a lot of hustle and bustle inside. That old feeling of being left out came over him. He waited in the hallway just outside the kitchen door, listening.

"Oh, Mama, you didn't," Evelyn shouted.

"Oh, but I did. I had a wonderful sale today, and that means a big bonus."

"Oh, great," Hadiya said, happily. "Now I can get my bicycle fixed."

His mama and two sisters all talked at the same time. When he finally walked in, everything stopped. Dead silence. All eyes turned on him.

"So?" he asked, not waiting for them to question where he had been, why he was late. He glanced at Hadiya and was tempted to return her smile, but turned away instead.

"So it's about time you got home," Evelyn said. She took charge while their mama worked each day.

Justin spread his legs as if to take a firm stand. He hated Evelyn being the boss. He stared ahead and said nothing.

"See how he acts, Mama," Evelyn said. "He's that way all the time."

"Aw, Evelyn," Hadiya said, to protect Justin.

He liked Hadiya. Everyone said they looked alike: both dark, tall, and thin. Hadiya, two years older than Justin and three years younger than Evelyn, was the tallest. At ten years old, Justin was already almost as tall as Evelyn.

Evelyn went on, "He gets in here just

[4]

before you every day, Mama. And he does nothing around here.''

Justin lowered his eyes but still said nothing.

"And you ought to see his room. Like Grandpa's pig pen,'' Evelyn said.

Hadiya giggled. Justin cut his eyes on her. She retreated to set the table.

Finally Mama said, "Justin, where have you been?''

"At the playground,'' he answered.

"Every day, Mama. That's all he does.''

"All right, Evelyn. I'll handle it,'' Mama said.

"But you always say you'll handle it and Justin gets away with murder,'' Evelyn said.

"That's enough, Evelyn.'' Mama increased her firmness.

Justin smiled inside, glad his mother had rescued him as she always did. He looked at Evelyn as if to say, *You know I'm her favorite.* Then he felt put out with himself for getting home too late to help with the groceries. He had let his mother down. He waited for her to say something about his being late.

[5]

His mama said nothing as she took lettuce, tomatoes, cucumbers, and sprouts from the refrigerator to make a salad for dinner. Justin still waited. Finally she said, "Go wash up."

On Tuesdays they had Justin's favorite dinner: pizza. At the dining table everyone seemed pleasant. Hadiya talked about a new recipe she just had to try. Justin thought he had weathered the storm when Evelyn offered him half her share of pizza because she was starting a new diet. And he knew things were back to normal when Hadiya offered to do the dishes. They all knew she wanted the kitchen to begin her messy cooking experiments.

Mama had other plans. "No, Hadiya, not tonight. Justin is going to do the dishes."

Justin looked at his mother and smiled shyly. Now he could make up for being late.

"Oh, no!" Evelyn cried. "Mama, you know he'll do nothing but make a mess that I'll have to clean up."

Justin flared with anger, knowing that

[6]

Evelyn always complained about his using too much soap, about his not rinsing dishes well and splashing water all over. "Aw, shut up!" he shouted. "Who can't wash dishes?"

"You!" Evelyn retorted. "We'll be tasting soap for days."

"Evelyn!" Mama said with quiet force. "Leave him alone. He has to learn. And, Justin, tomorrow I want you home so you can clean your room. Papa is coming."

"Grandpa's coming?" Justin jumped up from the table. "Wow! When?" Grandpa was his favorite person.

"Yes. Tomorrow, and I want your room clean. I want you to help Evelyn, too. You do whatever she tells you."

Justin glanced at Evelyn whose eyes fastened on him, sizing him up. He felt trapped, grounded. How would he ever get away with Anthony to play one-on-one? Moving slowly, taking his time, he cleared the table. As he let hot water run over the dishes, he thought, *Wish I could go live with Grandpa.*

# 2

## WOMEN'S WORK

JUSTIN WOKE EARLY. He had to clean his room and be ready when Anthony came by. If he cleaned up, then maybe Evelyn would let him go to the playground.

He looked about his room and decided there was no way he could be through by the time Anthony came. Suddenly he had an idea.

Justin knew Evelyn's one weakness: she liked to sleep late. In a very quiet house she might sleep all morning. With her asleep, he could slip away and play one-on-one with Anthony for an hour, at least.

First he took the phone off the hook. Suddenly he realized he had better catch Hadiya before she went into the kitchen and started banging around doing her experiments. He knew she liked reading in her room almost as much as she liked cooking. Especially if the books were about magic.

Luckily on his recent visit to the library he had checked out some books on just that subject. Now armed with those books on magic, he knocked on Hadiya's door.

She was already dressed. "Now what?" she asked as she opened the door.

"Can I come in?"

Seeing the books, she said, "No, you can't read in my room today."

He smiled. He liked reading in her room better than anywhere else in the house. She had a place for everything and everything was in its place. Her bed was always smoothly made. Her room reeked with order.

"I'm not here to read in your room," he said proudly. "You want these books?"

She looked at him suspiciously. "What do you want, Justin?"

He laughed. "Nothing. Here, girl. Read." He shoved the books at her.

She took them and quickly closed her door. He sighed, relieved.

Now with quiet assured, Evelyn would stay asleep and he could slip away to the playground. Softly, quickly, he went past her room down the hall. Just as he was almost to the door, the doorbell rang. "Oh, no!" he muttered. *Who's so stupid, hanging on the doorbell*, he thought. He raced to check.

"Anthony! Why you ringing the bell, man?"

"I wanted you to know I'm here."

"*Sh, sh, sh!*" Justin said.

"What's wrong?" Anthony wanted to know.

"I'm grounded. I think I can slip away, though. For a little while."

"Justin," Evelyn called. "Who is it?"

"Aw, shucks! She's alive. C'mon in." He shouted to Evelyn, "It's my friend."

"You know what Mama said," Evelyn called.

"You know what Mama said," he mimicked her under his breath to Anthony. Then he shouted, "I ain't going nowhere."

"You can't go to the playground?" Anthony asked.

"I told you I'm grounded. My grandpa's coming. Got to clean my room. C'mon."

With Anthony he felt comfortable even though his room was messy. The bed, though made, was lumpy. Covers showed beneath the bedspread. His closet door stood ajar. Clothes, more off hangers than on, were wedged together. Socks, balls, clothes hangers, and some T-shirts were scattered over the floor. Quickly he closed the closet door and said, "Sit down, man."

Anthony removed clothing from the chair and sat. Any other time Justin would not have been any more aware of his room than Anthony seemed now. But Justin was uneasy, ashamed, remembering the talk last night. *Like Grandpa's pig pen* flashed

[11]

into his mind. "Sisters," he blurted out. "Git on your nerves, man."

"I don't have any sisters," Anthony said as though he liked it that way. "But my mama and my grandma get on me. Wanting me to do their work."

"Yeah. Washing dishes, cleaning up, folding clothes."

"All that old stuff. Women's work. I hate it," Anthony said.

Justin heard Evelyn in her room. He knew those sounds of making the bed, straightening up. "They waste a lot of time cleaning, don't they?" he said. "And so many other things in the world to do." His foot shuffled a basketball left in the middle of the floor. "Let's play some one-on-one here," he said to Anthony.

Evelyn walked from her room just as they started out with the ball. "Where you think you're going?"

"Out," Justin replied.

"You had better get busy cleaning your room."

"Aw, c'mon, Evelyn! I got all day to clean." He and Anthony went to the backyard. Justin's father had put up a basketball net on the garage only months before he had been killed in an automobile accident. That had been four years ago when Justin was six years old. Justin still remembered playing one-on-one with his father. At first, when his father died, Justin couldn't play one-on-one at all because of a lonely heaviness in his chest. But now he hardly remembered anything except the fun he had had playing with his dad.

Justin played basketball with a lot of zest. However, Anthony, though shorter than Justin by almost three inches, was the better player. Justin jumped higher than Anthony, but Justin did not move as fast, nor did he keep as sharp an eye on the basket.

The sun shone hot, but they played hard and fast with Justin forgetting he had work to do.

Finally, exhausted, they took time out to get a cool drink from the water hose. Before the game started again, Evelyn bounded outside with her quick stride. "Play you both one-on-one," she challenged them.

"You mean one-on-two," Justin said, bouncing the ball.

"I'll beat both of you is what I mean," she said, and moved in on Justin, who still had the ball.

Evelyn was a fast, aggressive player. The two boys played as hard and as well as they knew how, but she still outscored them.

Finally she said, "Enough. Anthony, you go home now so Justin can do his work."

"You can't tell my friend what to do," Justin said.

"Then I'll tell you. You had better come in and do your work." Evelyn went inside.

"C'mon, Anthony, we don't have to do what she says." They started another game.

Evelyn shouted to Justin, "You want me to call Mama on the phone? You know what she told you last night."

Justin fumed with anger. "You'd better not." He knew they must never disturb their mother at the shop where she worked framing paintings and selling frames and artwork. Only for the most important things did they call.

[14]

"Listen, Anthony," he said, embarrassed. "I gotta go in and clean up."

"Want me to help?"

"Can you?" Justin asked, putting his hands on Anthony's shoulders. He knew he needed someone to help him get that room straight. He didn't want to ask Hadiya, and he wasn't about to let Evelyn know it was all beyond his skills. Maybe he and Anthony, together, could find a way to make his room neater. Maybe his bed could look as smooth and his closet as organized as Hadiya's. He even felt excited about that possibility.

For a moment they stood in the middle of the room. Anthony looked around. "You do need help," he said.

They began by stripping all the covers off the bed. They stumbled over each other as they tugged and pulled at the sheets and light blanket. They worked and worked.

Finally Anthony said, "Is that good?"

Justin thought of Hadiya's bed and felt that his did not look the way he had hoped it would. He tried again to tuck the sheets

[15]

and blanket underneath the bedspread. He patted the pillow. Though he knew the bed looked even worse than before, he sighed and said, "Yeah, it's OK. Fine. Now let's do the closet."

"When my grandma helps me clean my room, she makes me take everything out of the closet. You better get a broom," Anthony said.

When Justin returned with the broom, all the clothes from the closet were piled on his bed. Shoes, socks, balls, even games he had stored in back of his closet were strewn about the room.

*Anthony doesn't know any more than I do about getting closets neat,* Justin thought.

He got busy sweeping the closet floor, wondering how he would ever get all that stuff put away before Grandpa came.

It was well past lunchtime and they had only half of the things back in place. Exhausted and starving, Justin finally decided that his room looked no better than at first. And with the balls, socks, and extra clothes hangers strewn about outside

[16]

the closet, maybe it looked even worse. He jabbed his hands into his pockets and sighed. Why couldn't he get his room straight?

His mind flashed to Hadiya's room. *Neat as a pin.* Evelyn was not fussy as Hadiya, but her room was far neater than Justin now thought his would ever be.

He looked at Anthony sitting on the lumpy bed, with his elbows on his knees, his hands cupping his face.

"Let's stop now and get some lunch."

Anthony quickly said, "I gotta go home now."

Justin suddenly knew that Anthony had to be feeling as exhausted, frustrated, and disappointed as he was. He remembered Anthony's words about women's work. *Maybe this* is *work that only women and girls can do*, he thought, and went to see Anthony out. "We'll play tomorrow, OK?" he said.

"I can't. We're going away for the weekend. My family."

Justin said goodbye and went to the kitchen to find something to eat.

# 3

## GRANDPA ARRIVES

HE FOUND HADIYA in the kitchen. Whatever she was cooking smelled delicious.
*For a twelve-year-old, she cooks good*, he
thought. She should. She lived in the
kitchen, forever stirring up something.

"How come you always in the kitchen?"
he asked as he fixed himself a bowl of
cereal.

"I guess because I like magic."

"What's magic got to do with it?"

"Well, see, when I put dough in the
oven, what do I take out? Cake! And when

[19]

I put milk, eggs, sugar, and vanilla in a pot—add a little heat—presto! Pudding."

After he had downed two bowls of cereal and a peanut butter sandwich, he was still hungry. "M-mm-m, that smells good, Hadiya. What is it?"

Pleased, she said, "Want a taste?"

He licked the spoon. Lemon-flavored something. Only Hadiya knew what. Justin only knew it tasted good, and he wanted more.

"No," she said. "That's for dessert tonight. Grandpa's coming, remember?"

Justin knew he had to have something else to eat. "How about making me an egg?" he asked Hadiya.

"I'm through in the kitchen now. You can make your own egg."

"But I don't know how."

"Justin, that's the easiest thing in the world to make."

He had seen his mother scramble eggs with rice. They almost always had cooked rice in the refrigerator. He'd make eggs and rice.

When the teaspoon of butter was hot in

the small iron skillet, he added the rice first. He got the egg and a bowl ready to beat the egg for scrambling. He broke the egg and suddenly it seemed alive. He had no control. It fell from the shell so fast he didn't know what had happened. It splattered against the cabinet and slopped down onto the floor.

He grabbed paper towels and tried to quickly get it cleaned up. But the egg slipped all over. What a mess! Then he smelled something awful. The rice. It was smoking, almost on fire.

Just then Evelyn burst into the kitchen. "Justin, what in the world?"

"I'm hungry."

"You know you can't cook. Look at this floor. Get out!"

"I-I—let me get it up."

"No, get out, go!"

He left, no longer wanting more to eat. He stood outside the kitchen just long enough to hear Evelyn say, "Can't do a thing right."

He slammed his door and threw the clothing that remained on his bed across the room. He stormed around angrily kicking shoes, balls, his games. He wanted to scream, *I don't care how messy I am!*

Throwing himself across his bed, he lay with his feet dangling to the floor. He looked up at the light beige ceiling—the only uncluttered space in his room. Besides all the clutter on the floor, his walls, slightly darker than the ceiling, had every inch of space covered. Pictures of baseball, basketball, and football players competed with rock stars, TV stars. And he had just added a big picture of Halley's Comet, his favorite at the moment.

Now he kept his eye on the ceiling, trying to forget Evelyn and how much he still had to do to make his room look neat.

A flood of light woke him. At first he thought he was dreaming. His mama, Hadiya, Evelyn, and his grandpa were all in his room.

"Justin, wake up. Grandpa is here," his mama said.

At first he was dazed. Then suddenly he realized they *were* there—in all that clutter.

"What happened in here?" his mama asked. Her quiet manner and even disposition slipped away. "Why didn't you clean your room?" she asked sharply.

He couldn't raise his eyes, but he felt their gazes on him. He became angry. *Why did they bring Grandpa into my room?* he wondered. He refused to answer his mother's question.

"I'll tell you, Mama. He played. Then he messed up the kitchen."

"Evelyn, keep quiet," Hadiya said, as if embarrassed to have that said in front of Grandpa.

"Why you always have to put your mouth in it?" Justin shouted. "I don't like you telling me what to do. I don't like doing women's work."

"What's womanish about cleaning this room?" Evelyn retorted.

"*I* told you to clean your room. Evelyn didn't," Mama said. "What's wrong with you, Justin?"

"Wait a minute," Grandpa finally said. "Why don't all of you leave me and Justin alone for a little while."

[23]

"But, Papa . . ." Mama said.

"Go on now," Grandpa insisted.

"All right," Mama said, "but you're going to clean this room, you hear me, Justin." She threw up her hands as she left with Evelyn and Hadiya.

Alone with his grandpa, he wanted to fling himself into Grandpa's arms. He loved Grandpa more than anyone. But he sat on his bed unable to move. Unable to speak. He struggled to hold back rising tears. Grandpa stood waiting.

Finally Justin said, "I can't stand it here. I can't do anything right. Nothing." The tears splashed and he quickly brushed them away with the back of his hand. He burned with shame: his grandpa seeing him cry like a baby.

Grandpa still waited quietly. That's what Justin liked about him. Grandpa didn't rush him. He listened. Justin went on, "I don't like to clean house, Grandpa. I don't like to wash dishes and I hate folding clothes."

"And to make your bed, pick up your things, and to tidy up your room, eh?"

[24]

Suddenly Justin was again aware of how messy his room looked.

His grandpa reached out and touched his shoulder. When Justin looked up, he saw that look on his grandpa's face that was always there after a great joke. They both burst out laughing.

"How would you like to come home to

the ranch with me? It's festival time again."

Justin beamed. He loved the big rodeo, the games, and the parade in Grandpa's town.

"You know those Black cowboys I've been telling you about? Their rodeo is performing."

"You're kidding, Grandpa."

"I kid you not."

"Can I *really* come?" Justin asked.

"Let's ask your mama." He winked at Justin.

His mama did not look up when she said, "I'm upset with Justin. He will not go any place until that room is neat."

"All right, all right, I'll clean my room." He raced to his room and quickly stuffed all the things back into the closet and closed the closet door.

When his mama came to see what he had done, he nervously tried to smooth his bed, hoping she wouldn't open the closet door.

His mother looked around the room and sighed. Justin was not sure he had passed inspection.

Soon they all sat down to Hadiya's delicious spaghetti dinner.

While they waited for that dessert Justin had tasted, Grandpa asked again if Justin could come home with him for a few days.

"I don't know, Papa," Mama said.

"Grandpa, why don't you take me?" Hadiya asked. "I'd cook you some good food."

"If you cook for me the way you cooked tonight, I'd get fat, Diya. It's Justin's turn. Yours is next. How about it, Daughter?"

"Justin, do you think you deserve to go?" Mama asked.

"Oh, Mama, let him go. Be good to get rid of him for a while," Evelyn said.

"Sure, I want to go," Justin said. He looked at Evelyn as if to say, *I won't miss you either.*

"He can go, but only if you spend the night, Papa," Mama said.

"That's a deal," Grandpa said.

"Yeah, yeah, yeah," went up around the table, and Hadiya went to serve her magic dessert.

[27]

# ♫ 4 ♫

## A VISIT TO Q-T RANCH

•

LATER THAT EVENING Justin packed his duffel bag. He polished his cowboy boots and shined his silver cowboy belt buckle. He was so excited about going with Grandpa he couldn't sleep.

He turned restlessly on his bed, thinking about the festival and the rodeo. He thought of the horses at Grandpa's ranch. Three of them in all. One was called Cropper after the horse of the famous cowboy Bill Pickett. Another horse, a dapple gray, got his name from Grandpa. Grandpa said the horse talked to him, so he named him Palaver. Black Lightning, the youngest of the three, belonged to Justin whenever Justin visited the ranch. Justin called him Black and called Palaver, Pal.

For as long as he could remember, the Q–T Ranch had been in his mother's family. Justin's Great-Great-Grandfather Ward had been a cowboy who rode cattle trails taking cattle to market, out of Texas into Kansas. Those trips lasted many weeks, sometimes months. People in the East depended upon cowboys to put beef on their tables.

Then the railroads spread across the country linking the East and West. Cowboys were no longer needed to drive cattle. So, many of them settled in the West. Great-Great-Grandpa Ward settled in Missouri. He founded a ranch with a hundred and sixty acres. The place was so quiet and tranquil, he named it the Q–T Ranch.

Now Justin's house creaked in the stillness. Everyone else was asleep. Justin lay on his bed imagining himself riding upon a horse under a dark starlit sky.

Thousands of cattle rested close by. He listened to their breathing. Cowboys lay on blankets scattered about on the ground. Justin carefully guided his horse around the men. Snores of some rattled in the darkness while some slept without a sound of breathing.

The chuck wagon that carried supplies and the cook's utensils stood farther ahead on the trail. A big box attached to the wagon held the iron rods that fitted over a firepit, and a table. When it was time to cook, cowboys helped lift the rods from the box and unfold the cook's table.

Justin imagined now that the cook lay sleeping under the wagon. A lantern attached to the back of the wagon burned brightly, protecting the supplies from animals. Cowboys had mostly sourdough biscuits, dried beef, and beans. That was their main food, day in and day out, for months on the trail.

Justin went on imagining. He saw himself riding, keeping an eye on the cattle, singing softly. He looked at the stars to tell the time of night. Only one more hour for him to ride. Soon another cowboy would relieve him. Far away on the horizon bright orange lightning flashed. The cattle moved restlessly. Justin kept up his song. Singing soothed the cattle, made them calm. He wanted no stampede tonight.

Justin's house was quiet and still. Wishing he could fall asleep, Justin listened to a dog barking far away. His mind wandered back to the cattle trail he imagined. He went on riding and singing.

Finally the stars told him his watch was over. Another cowboy came to ride around the herd and sing.

Justin saw himself falling on his bedroll, ready to sleep but still worried about the restless cattle. He dozed. Then suddenly he heard cattle lowing. Hoofbeats sounded wildly on the trail. A stampede! Quickly Justin got up, jumped onto his horse, and rode to head off the leader of the cattle. He had to turn that leader toward the tail end of the herd. Other cowboys were now up and on their horses riding with him. They rode hard and fast, circling the cattle, settling them down again.

Now Justin tossed on his bed, so exhausted he fell asleep.

The next morning the house buzzed with excitement. Justin was anxious to go, impatient with all the talk and attention centered on Grandpa. Hadiya insisted on packing a lunch. Mama brought out a box of mended socks and shirts that Grandpa had left on the last trip. She also gave Grandpa vitamins, soap, and oils, which she insisted Grandpa use. Justin doubted that Grandpa would use the smelly cologne Mama tried to shove off on him.

"Here," Mama said. "Use this and wow the ladies." She laughed.

"I don't need stuff like that to wow ladies," he said, handing it back to her.

But Mama had her way. She tucked the cologne into the box with the other things. Finally they loaded the truck that Grandpa called his "Iron Pony." They started on their way. Already it was hot, and the day promised to be a scorcher.

[32]

It pleased Justin that they were taking the long way. The highway wound high up around curves, then down again to the plains near the foot of the rolling hills. By lunchtime they still had some miles to go. "I know just the place for our lunch," Grandpa said.

The truck hummed up a steep grade. Then Grandpa turned off onto a narrow dirt road. Soon they came to a parking spot. Grandpa got out and suggested that Justin carry the lunch.

Together they walked on a trail that led into cool woods. Justin was hungry. They walked and walked, often giving way to people coming down the trail.

On they went, away from the regular trail onto a small path. Finally Grandpa said, "Here we are."

Justin looked around and breathed a sigh of happiness. The silence was peaceful. It was as if no other people had been there. He remembered the fallen tree that made a natural seat for them. The log lay in the quiet clearing with big trees growing around. Justin lifted his eyes to only a small circle of silvery sky. He felt small peeking through the skylight of those big trees.

Hadiya had made sandwiches with lots of lettuce and sprouts. At home he would not have eaten that green stuff. But growling hungry now, he ate it all.

Justin also remembered a lake nearby. "Can we walk to the lake, Grandpa?"

Grandpa smiled, glad that Justin had asked. The lake was one of his favorite places, too.

When they returned to the main trail, more people joined them going toward the lake. Justin was pleased that his grandpa, a good hiker, walked as fast as he. Justin liked to move quickly on a trail.

Soon they saw the lake sparkling in the bright sun. People fished and some splashed their feet in the cool water. Justin and his grandpa walked around to the far side enjoying the sounds of birds and small lapping waves, and the smell of growing things.

They came upon a man fishing. The man looked like he was somebody's grandpa, too. He spoke warmly to Justin and asked,

"Are you going fishing today, young man?"

"Not today," Justin replied. "We're here for just a little while."

"Having any luck?" Grandpa asked the man.

"Lots. But I don't like fish. I just like fishing." The man and Grandpa laughed.

"Don't like fish?" Justin asked. "I like fish and fishing."

"Then you may have these." The man held up a string of four speckled trout, gleaming in colors of the rainbow.

Justin grinned and said, "Thanks!" With the string of fish, Justin and Grandpa circled the lake. When they were back near the trail leading from the lake, they shouted to the fisherman and waved goodbye. Soon they were on the road again, heading to the Q–T Ranch.

# ⟡ 5 ⟡

## MAKING A BED IS EASY

GRANDPA'S HOUSE SAT about a mile in from the road. Between that road and the house lay a large meadow with a small stream. Everything seemed in order when Justin and Grandpa arrived.

Justin got out and opened the gate to the winding road that led toward the house. The meadow below shimmered in waves of tall green grass. The horses grazed calmly there. Justin was so excited to see them again that he waved his grandpa on. "I'll walk up, Grandpa." He ran down into the meadow.

[36]

Pink prairie roses blossomed near the fence. Goldenrod, sweet william, and black-eyed susans added color here and there. Justin waded through the lush green grass.

The horses, drinking at the stream, paid no attention as he raced across the meadow toward them. *Cropper looks so old*, he thought as he came closer. But Black Lightning's coat shone, as beautiful as ever. Justin gave a familiar whistle. The horses lifted their heads and their ears went back, but only Black moved toward him on the run.

Justin reached up and Black lowered his head. Justin rubbed him behind the ear. Softly he said, "Good boy, Black. I've missed you. You glad to see me?"

Then Pal nosed in, wanting to be petted, too. Cropper didn't bother. Justin wondered if Cropper's eyesight was fading.

The sun had moved well toward the west. Long shadows from the rolling hills reached across the plains. "Want to take me home, boy?" Justin asked Black.

Black lowered his head and pawed with one foot as he shook his mane. Justin led him to a large rock. From the rock, Justin straddled Black's back, without a saddle. Black walked him home.

Grandpa's house stood on a hill surrounded by plains, near the rolling hills. Over many years, trees standing close by the house had grown tall and strong. The house, more than a hundred years old, was made of logs. The sun and rain had turned the logs on the outside an iron gray. Flecks of green showed in some of the logs.

When Justin went inside, Grandpa had already changed his clothes. Now he busily measured food for the animals. While Grandpa was away, a neighbor had come to feed the pigs and chickens. The horses took care of themselves, eating and drinking in the meadow. Today the horses would have some oats, too.

"Let's feed the animals first," Grandpa said. "Then we'll cook those fish for dinner. You can clean them when we get back."

Justin sighed deeply. How could he tell Grandpa he didn't know how to clean fish?

[38]

He was sure to make a mess of it. Worriedly, he helped Grandpa load the truck with the food and water for the chickens and pigs. They put in oats for the horses, too. Then they drove to the chicken yard.

As they rode along the dusty road, Justin remembered Grandpa telling him that long, long ago they had raised hundreds of cattle on Q–T Ranch. Then when Justin's mama was a little girl, they had raised only chickens on the ranch, selling many eggs to people in the cities. Now Grandpa had only a few chickens, three pigs, and three horses.

At the chicken yard, chickens rushed around to get the bright yellow corn that Justin threw to them. They fell over each other, fluttering and clucking. While Justin fed them, Grandpa gathered the eggs.

The pigs lazily dozed in their pens. They had been wallowing in the mud. pond nearby. Now cakes of dried mud dotted their bodies. The floor where they slept had mud on it, too. Many flies buzzed around. *My room surely doesn't look like this*, Justin thought.

[39]

The pigs ran to the trough when Grandpa came with the pail of grain mixed with water. They grunted and snorted. The smallest one squealed with delight. *He's cute*, Justin thought.

By the time they had fed the horses oats and returned home, it was dark and cooler. Justin was glad it was so late. Maybe now Grandpa would clean the fish so that they could eat sooner. He was hungry.

Grandpa had not changed the plan. He gave Justin some old newspapers, a small sharp knife, and a bowl with clean water.

"Now," he said, handing Justin the pail that held the fish, "you can clean these."

Justin looked at the slimy fish in the water. How could he tell his grandpa that he didn't want to touch those fish? He still didn't want Grandpa to know that he had never cleaned fish before. Evelyn's words crowded him: *Can't do anything right.* He dropped his shoulders and sighed. "Do I have to, Grandpa?"

"We have to eat, don't we?"

"But—but I don't know how," Justin cried.

[40]

"Oh, it's not hard. I'll show you." Grandpa placed a fish on the newspaper. "Be careful now and keep it on this paper. When you're all done, just fold the paper and all the mess is inside."

Justin watched Grandpa scrape the fish upward from the tail toward the head. Little shiny scales came off easily. Then he cut the fish's belly upward from a little vent hole and scraped all the stuff inside onto the paper. "Now see how easy that is. You try," Grandpa said. "Be very careful with the knife." He watched Justin to see if he knew what to do.

Justin scraped the tiny scales off confidently. Then he hesitated. Screwing up his face, he shuddered as he cut, then pulled the insides out. Finally he got the knack of it.

Grandpa, satisfied that Justin would do fine, went into the kitchen to make a fire in the big stove.

Later that evening, Justin felt proud when Grandpa let him put the fish on the table.

After dinner, they sat in the living room

[41]

near the huge fireplace. Great-Great-Grandma Ward had used that same fireplace to cook her family's meals.

Justin looked at the fireplace, trying to imagine how it must have been then. *How did people cook without a stove?* He knew Grandpa's stove was nothing like his mama's. Once that big iron stove got hot there was no way to turn it off or to low or to simmer. You just set the pots in a cooler place on the back of Grandpa's stove.

"Grandpa, how did your grandma cook bread in this fireplace?" he asked.

"Cooking bread in this fireplace was easy for my grandma. She once had to bake her bread on a hoe."

"But a hoe is for making a garden, Grandpa."

"Yes, I know, and it was that kind of hoe that she used. She chopped cotton with her hoe down in Tennessee. There was no fireplace in the family's little one-room house, so she cooked with a fire outside. She had no nice iron pots and skillets like I have now in the kitchen.

"At night when the family came in from

the cotton fields, Grandma made a simple bread with cornmeal and a little flour. She patted it and dusted it with more flour. Then she put it on the iron hoe and stuck it in the ashes. When it was nice and brown the ashes brushed off easily."

"How did they ever get from Tennessee to Missouri?"

"Justin, I've told you that so many times."

"I know, Grandpa. But I like to hear it. Tell me again."

"As a boy, my grandpa was a slave. Right after slavery my grandpa worked on a ranch in Tennessee. He rode wild mustangs and tamed them to become good riding horses. He cared so much about horses, he became a cowboy.

"He got married and had a family. Still he left home for many weeks, sometimes months, driving thousands of cattle over long trails. Then he heard about the government giving away land in the West through the Homestead Act. You only had to build a house and live in it to keep the land."

[43]

"So my great-great-grandpa built this house." Justin stretched out on the floor. He looked around at the walls that were now dark brown from many years of smoke from the fireplace.

"Just the room we're in now," Grandpa said. "I guess every generation of Wards has added something. Now, my daddy, Phillip, added on the kitchen and the room right next to this one that is the dining room.

"I built the bathroom and the rooms upstairs. Once we had a high loft. I guess you'd call it an attic. I made that into those rooms upstairs. So you see, over the years this house has grown and grown. Maybe when you're a man, you'll bring your family here," Grandpa said.

"I don't know. Maybe. But I'd have to have an electric kitchen."

"As I had to have a bathroom with a shower. Guess that's progress," Grandpa said, and laughed.

"Go on, Grandpa. Tell me what it was like when Great-Great-Grandpa first came to Missouri."

"I think it's time for us to go to bed."

"It's not that late," Justin protested.

"For me it is. We'll have to get up early. I'll have to ride fence tomorrow. You know, in winter Q–T Ranch becomes a feeder ranch for other people's cattle. In spring, summer, and early fall cattle roam and graze in the high country. In winter when the heavy frosts come and it's bitter cold, they return to the plains. Many of those cattle feed at Q–T. I have to have my fences mended before fall so the cattle can't get out."

"Can I ride fence with you?" Justin asked.

"Sure you can. Maybe you'll like riding fence. That's a man's work." Grandpa laughed.

Justin remembered that conversation in his room about women's work, and the tears. He burned with shame. He didn't laugh.

Upstairs, Grandpa gave Justin sheets and a blanket for his bed. "It'll be cool before morning," he told Justin. "You'll need this blanket. Can you make your bed?"

Justin frowned. He hated making his

[45]

bed. But he looked at Grandpa and said, "I'm no baby." Justin joined Grandpa in laughter.

Grandpa went to his room. When he was all ready for bed, he came and found Justin still struggling to make his bed. Those sheets had to be made nice and smooth to impress Grandpa, Justin thought, but it wasn't easy.

Grandpa watched. "Want to see how a man makes a bed?" Grandpa asked.

Justin didn't answer. Grandpa waited. Finally, Justin, giving up, said, "Well, all right."

"Let's do it together," Grandpa said. "You on the other side."

Grandpa helped him smooth the bottom sheet and tuck it under the mattress at the head and foot of the bed. Then he put on the top sheet and blanket and smoothed them carefully.

"Now, let's tuck those under the mattress only at the foot of the bed," he said.

"That's really neat, Grandpa," Justin said, impressed.

"That's not it, yet. We want it to stay

[46]

neat, don't we? Now watch." Grandpa carefully folded the covers in equal triangles and tucked them so that they made a neat corner at the end of the mattress. "Now do your side exactly the way I did mine."

Soon Justin was in bed. When Grandpa tucked him in, he asked, "How does it feel?"

Justin flexed his toes and ankles. "Nice. Snug."

"Like a bug in a rug?"

Justin laughed. Then Grandpa said, "That's how a *man* makes a bed."

Still laughing, Justin asked, "Who taught *you* how to make a bed? Your grandpa?"

"No. My grandma." Grandpa grinned and winked at Justin. "Good night."

Justin lay listening to the winds whispering in the trees. Out of his window in the darkness he saw lightning bugs flashing, heard crickets chirping. But before the first hoot of an owl, he was fast asleep.

## 6

# RIDING FENCE

THE SMELL OF COFFEE and home-smoked ham woke Justin. His grandpa was already up and downstairs cooking breakfast. Justin jumped out of bed and quickly put on his clothes.

Grandpa had hot pancakes, apple jelly, and ham all ready for the table. Justin ate two stacks of pancakes with two helpings of everything else.

After breakfast, Grandpa cleared the table, preparing to wash the dishes. "Would you rather wash or dry?" he asked Justin.

"Neither," Justin replied, quickly thinking how little success he had with dishes.

Grandpa said nothing as he removed the dishes from the table. He took his time, carefully measuring liquid soap and letting hot water run in the sink. Then he washed each dish and rinsed it with care, too. No water splashed or spilled. Soapsuds were not all over. How easy it looked, the way Grandpa did it.

After washing the dishes, Grandpa swept the floor and then went upstairs.

Justin stood around downstairs. He had a strange feeling of guilt and wished he had helped with the dishes. He heard Grandpa moving about, above in his room. Justin thought of going outside, down into the meadow, but he decided to see what was going on upstairs.

When he saw his grandpa busy making his own big bed, Justin went into his room. His unmade bed and his pajamas on the floor bothered him. But he decided that the room didn't look too bad. He picked up his pajamas and placed them on the bed and sat beside them. He waited.

Finally Grandpa came in and said, "Are you riding fence with me today?"

"Oh yes!"

"Fine. But why don't you make your bed? You'll probably feel pretty tired tonight. A well-made bed can be a warm welcome."

Justin moved slowly, reluctant to let Grandpa see him struggle with the bed. He started. What a surprise! Everything was tightly in place. He only had to smooth the covers. The bed was made. No lumps and bumps. Justin looked at Grandpa and grinned broadly. "That was easy!" he shouted.

"Don't you think you should unpack your clothes? They won't need ironing if you hang them up. You gotta look razor sharp for the festival." He gave Justin some clothes hangers.

"Are we *really* going to the festival every day?" Justin asked.

"You bet, starting with the judging early tomorrow and the dance tomorrow night." Grandpa winked at him.

Justin's excitement faded when he started

[51]

unpacking his rumpled shirts. "They sure are wrinkled, Grandpa," he said.

"Maybe that's because they weren't folded."

"I can't ever get them folded right," Justin cried.

"Well, let's see. Turn it so the buttons face down." Grandpa showed Justin how to bring the sleeves to the back, turning in the sides so that the sleeves were on top. Then he folded the tail of the shirt over the cuffs, and made a second fold up to the collar. "Now you try it."

Justin tried it. "Oh, I see. That was easy, Grandpa." Justin smiled, pleased with himself.

"Everything's easy when you know how."

Justin, happy with his new-found skill, hurriedly placed his clothes on the hangers. He hoped the wrinkles would disappear in time for the festival.

"Now you'll look sharp," Grandpa said.

Justin felt a surge of love for his grandpa. He would always remember how to make a bed snug as a bug and fold clothes neatly.

He grabbed Grandpa's hand. They walked downstairs, still holding hands, to get ready to ride fence.

Riding fence meant inspecting the fence all around the ranch to see where it needed mending. Riding fence took a great deal of a rancher's time. Justin and Grandpa planned to spend most of the day out on the plains. Grandpa said he'd pack a lunch for them to eat on the far side of the ranch.

Justin was surprised when Grandpa packed only flour, raisins, and chunks of smoked pork. Grandpa also packed jugs of water and makings for coffee.

The horses stood in the meadow as if they knew a busy day awaited them. While Grandpa saddled Pal, he let Justin finish the saddling of Black Lightning. Justin tightened the cinches on Black, feeling the strong pull on his arm muscles. With their supplies in their saddlebags, they mounted Pal and Black, leaving Cropper behind to graze in the meadow.

The early sun shone fiery red on the hilltops while the foothills were cast in shades of purple. The dew still lingered heavily on the morning. They let their horses canter away past the house through the tall green grass. But on the outer edge of the ranch where the fence started, they walked the horses at a steady pace.

The fence had three rows of taut wire. "That's a pretty high fence," Justin said.

"We have to keep the cattle in. But deer sometimes leap that fence and eat hay with the cattle." When it got bitter cold and frosty, Grandpa rode around the ranch dropping bales of hay for the cattle. It took a lot of hay to feed the cattle during the winter months.

"I didn't think a cow could jump very high," Justin said.

"Aw, come on. Surely you know that a cow jumped over the moon." Grandpa had a serious look on his face.

"I guess that's a joke, eh?" Justin laughed.

Justin noticed that Grandpa had a map. When they came to a place in the fence that looked weak, Grandpa marked it on his map. Later, helpers who came to do the work would know exactly where to mend. That saved time.

Now the sun heated up the morning. The foothills were now varying shades of green. Shadows dotted the plains. Among the blackish green trees on the rolling hills, fog still lingered like lazy clouds. Insects buzzed. A small cloud of mosquitoes swarmed just behind their heads, and beautiful cardinals splashed their redness on the morning air. Justin felt a surge of happiness and hugged Black with his knees and heels.

Suddenly he saw a doe standing close to the fence. "Look, Grandpa!" he said. She seemed alarmed but did not run away. Doe eyes usually look peaceful and sad, Justin remembered. Hers widened with fear. Then Justin saw a fawn caught in the wire of the fence.

Quickly they got off their horses. They hitched them to a post and moved cautiously toward the fawn.

The mother rushed to the fence but stopped just short of the sharp wire. "Stay back and still," Grandpa said to Justin.

"She doesn't know we will help her baby. She thinks we might hurt it. She wants to protect it."

The mother pranced restlessly. She pawed the ground, moving as close to the fence as she could. Near the post the fence had been broken. The wire curled there dangerously. The fawn's head, caught in the wire, bled close to an ear. Whenever it pulled its head the wire cut deeper.

Grandpa quickly untangled the fawn's head.

Blood flowed from the cut.

"Oh, Grandpa, it will die," Justin said sadly.

"No, no," Grandpa assured Justin. "Lucky we got here when we did. It hasn't been caught long."

The fawn moved toward the doe. The mother, as if giving her baby a signal, bounded off. The baby trotted behind.

As they mounted their horses, Justin suddenly felt weak in the stomach. Remembering the blood, he trembled. Black, too, seemed uneasy. He moved his nostrils nervously and strained against the bit. He arched his neck and sidestepped quickly. Justin pulled the reins. "Whoa, boy!"

"Let him run," Grandpa said.

Justin kicked Black's sides and off they raced across the plain. They ran and ran, Justin pretending he was rounding up cattle. Then Black turned and raced back toward Grandpa and Pal.

"Whoa, boy," Justin commanded. Justin felt better and Black seemed calm, ready now to go on riding fence.

[57]

# 7

## ABOUT BLACK COWBOYS

THE SUN BEAMED down and sweat rolled off Justin as he rode on with Grandpa, looking for broken wires in the fence. They were well away from the house, on the far side of the ranch. Flies buzzed around the horses and now gnats swarmed in clouds just above their heads. The prairie resounded with songs of the bluebirds, the bobwhite quails, and the mockingbirds mimicking them all. The cardinal's song, as lovely as any, included a whistle.

Justin thought of Anthony and how

Anthony whistled for Pepper, his dog.

It was well past noon and Justin was hungry. Soon they came upon a small, well-built shed, securely locked. Nearby was a small stream. Grandpa reined in his horse. When he and Justin dismounted, they hitched the horses, and unsaddled them.

"We'll have our lunch here," Grandpa said. Justin was surprised when Grandpa took black iron pots, other cooking utensils, and a table from the shed. Justin helped him remove some iron rods that Grandpa carefully placed over a shallow pit. These would hold the pots. Now Justin understood why Grandpa had brought uncooked food. They were going to cook outside.

First they collected twigs and cow dung. Grandpa called it cowchips. "These," Grandpa said, holding up a dried brown pad, "make the best fuel. Gather them up."

There were plenty of chips left from the cattle that had fed there in winter. Soon they had a hot fire.

Justin watched as Grandpa carefully

[59]

washed his hands and then began to cook their lunch.

"When I was a boy about your age, I used to go with my father on short runs with cattle. We'd bring them down from the high country onto the plains."

"Did you stay out all night?"

"Sometimes. And that was the time I liked most. The cook often made for supper what I am going to make for lunch."

Grandpa put raisins into a pot with a little water and placed them over the fire. Justin was surprised when Grandpa put flour in a separate pan. He used his fist to make a hole right in the middle of the flour. In that hole he placed some shortening. Then he added water. With his long delicate fingers he mixed the flour, water, and shortening until he had a nice round mound of dough.

Soon smooth circles of biscuits sat in an iron skillet with a lid on top. Grandpa put the skillet on the fire with some of the red-hot chips scattered over the lid.

Justin was amazed. How could only those ingredients make good bread? But he said nothing as Grandpa put the chunks of smoked pork in a skillet and started them cooking. Soon the smell was so delicious, Justin could hardly wait.

Finally Grandpa suggested that Justin take the horses to drink at the stream. "Keep your eyes open and don't step on any snakes."

Justin knew that diamondback rattlers sometimes lurked around. They were dangerous. He must be careful. He watered Black first.

While watering Pal, he heard rustling in the grass. His heart pounded. He heard the noise again. He wanted to run, but was too afraid. He looked around carefully. There were two black eyes staring at him. He tried to pull Pal away from the water, but Pal refused to stop drinking. Then Justin saw the animal. It had a long tail like a rat's. But it was as big as a cat. Then he saw something crawling on its back. They were little babies, hanging on as the animal ran.

*A mama opossum and her babies,* he thought, and was no longer afraid.

By the time the horses were watered, lunch was ready. *"M-mm-m,"* Justin said as he reached for a plate. The biscuits were golden brown, yet fluffy inside. And the sizzling pork was now crisp. Never had he eaten stewed raisins before.

"Grandpa, I didn't know you could cook like this," Justin said when he had tasted the food. "I didn't know men could cook so good."

"Why, Justin, some of the best cooks in the world are men."

Justin remembered the egg on the floor and his rice burning. The look he gave Grandpa revealed his doubts.

"It's true," Grandpa said. "All the cooks on the cattle trail were men. In hotels and restaurants they call them chefs."

"How did you make these biscuits?"

"That's a secret. One day I'll let you make some."

"Were you a cowboy, Grandpa?"

"I'm still a cowboy."

"No, you're not."

"Yes, I am. I work with cattle, so I'm a cowboy."

[62]

"You know what I mean. The kind who rides bulls, broncobusters. That kind of cowboy."

"No, I'm not that kind. But I know some."

"Are they famous?"

"No, but I did meet a real famous Black cowboy once. When I was eight years old, my grandpa took me to meet his friend Bill Pickett. Bill Pickett was an old man then. He had a ranch in Oklahoma."

"Were there lots of Black cowboys?"

"Yes. Lots of them. They were hard workers, too. They busted broncos, branded calves, and drove cattle. My grandpa tamed wild mustangs."

"Bet they were famous."

"Oh, no. Some were. Bill Pickett created the sport of bulldogging. You'll see that at the rodeo. One cowboy named Williams taught Rough Rider Teddy Roosevelt how to break horses; and another one named Clay taught Will Rogers, the comedian, the art of roping." Grandpa offered Justin the last biscuit.

When they had finished their lunch they

[63]

led the horses away from the shed to graze. As they watched the horses, Grandpa went on, "Now, there were some more very famous Black cowboys. Jessie Stahl. They say he was the best rider of wild horses in the West."

"How could he be? Nobody ever heard about him. I didn't."

"Oh, there're lots of famous Blacks you never hear or read about. You ever hear about Deadwood Dick?"

Justin laughed. "No."

"There's another one. His real name was Nate Love. He could outride, outshoot anyone. In Deadwood City in the Dakota Territory, he roped, tied, saddled, mounted, and rode a wild horse faster than anyone. Then in the shooting match, he hit the bull's-eye every time. The people named him Deadwood Dick right on the spot. Enough about cowboys, now. While the horses graze, let's clean up here and get back to our men's work."

Justin felt that Grandpa was still teasing him, the way he had in Justin's room when he had placed his hand on Justin's shoulder. There was still the sense of shame whenever the outburst about women's work and the tears were remembered.

As they cleaned the utensils and dishes, Justin asked, "Grandpa, you think housework is women's work?"

"Do you?" Grandpa asked quickly.

"I asked you first, Grandpa."

"I guess asking you that before I answer is unfair. No, I don't. Do you?"

"Well, it seems easier for them," Justin said as he splashed water all over, glad he was outside.

"Easier than for me?"

"Well, not for you, I guess, but for me, yeah."

"Could it be because you don't know how?"

"You mean like making the bed and folding the clothes."

"Yes." Grandpa stopped and looked at Justin. "Making the bed is easy now, isn't it? All work is that way. It doesn't matter who does the work, man or woman, when

[65]

it needs to be done. What matters is that we try to learn how to do it the best we can in the most enjoyable way."

"I don't think I'll ever like housework," Justin said, drying a big iron pot.

"It's like any other kind of work. The better you do it, the easier it becomes, and we seem not to mind doing things that are easy."

With the cooking rods and all the utensils put away, they locked the shed and went for their horses.

"Now, I'm going to let you do the cinches again. You'll like that."

*There's that teasing again*, Justin thought. "Yeah. That's a man's work," he said, and mounted Black.

"There are some good horsewomen. You'll see them at the rodeo." Grandpa mounted Pal. They went on their way, riding along silently, scanning the fence.

Finally Justin said, "I was just kidding, Grandpa." Then without planning to, he said, "I bet you don't like boys who cry like babies."

"Do I know any boys who cry like babies?"

"Aw, Grandpa, you saw me crying."

"Oh, I didn't think you were crying like a baby. In your room, you mean? We all cry sometime."

"You? Cry, Grandpa?"

"Sure."

They rode on, with Grandpa marking his map. Justin remained quiet, wondering what could make a man like Grandpa cry.

As if knowing Justin's thoughts, Grandpa said, "I remember crying when you were born."

"Why? Didn't you want me?"

"Oh, yes. You were the most beautiful baby. But, you see, your grandma, Beth, had just died. When I held you I was flooded with joy. Then I thought, *Grandma will never see this beautiful boy.* I cried."

The horses wading through the grass made the only sound in the silence. Then Grandpa said, "There's an old saying, son. 'The brave hide their fears, but share their tears.' Tears bathe the soul."

Justin looked at his grandpa. Their eyes caught. A warmth spread over Justin and he lowered his eyes. He wished he could tell his grandpa all he felt, how much he loved him.

# THE EXODUSTERS

THE HUMID HEAT did not let up and Justin was wet with sweat and worn out when they got back home. Not having been on a horse all summer, his legs were stiff. His backside was sore from the saddle. He could hardly walk. He welcomed Grandpa's suggestion that he take a shower and rest.

In the shower he let cool water pelt him hard. He thought about the lunch outside and the talk about cowboys. He could hardly wait for the festival and the rodeo.

When he went into his room to rest, he heard his grandpa downstairs getting ready to take his shower. He decided to go into Grandpa's room to look out at the wooded rolling hills. There were pictures of the whole family in Grandpa's room, too. Justin liked looking at them.

He liked best the old ones of Great-Grandpa Phillip Ward, Sr., with all of his sons. Justin noted that Evelyn was very much like him. Great-Grandpa Phillip Ward was not as tall as some of his sons. Justin's grandpa, Phillip Ward, Jr., was the tallest of them all. He and Hadiya looked like him.

There was another picture, of a man with a long rifle standing with his foot on a saddle. He had on cowboy boots with spurs, a cowboy hat, and cowboy clothes, including a kerchief around his neck. He was very tall with a serious look. That was Great-Great-Grandpa Wiley Ward who brought the family from Tennessee into Missouri after the slaves had been freed almost fifteen years.

Justin liked this room very much.

[70]

Grandpa's bed was big and high. Beside it stood an old treadle sewing machine used now as a small table. On top a brass lamp's highly polished metal shone brightly. Underneath were some very old books. Justin read the titles. One, *Reflections on My Young Life*, by Phillip Ward, Sr., captured his attention. Justin thumbed through pages. "How We Came to Missouri" caught his eye. He went into his room, lay on his bed, and began to read.

It was cold that winter, 1879. I was ten years old, but was allowed much responsibility. Talk about Negroes leaving the South and traveling West filled the air. We were not slaves, but neither were we free. Mama and Papa could not vote. They were denied land and for fear of being killed they dared not act for a better life.

It was that summer that I noticed Mama canning more berries, fruits, and vegetables. She and my sisters, Jennie and Erma, knitted heavier sweaters and socks for us all. They sewed flannel sheets and mended quilts.

Papa and my brothers, Julius, James and John (twins), and Silas, worked on shoeing our horses, repairing wagon wheels and

[71]

making new ones. They built strong boxes in which to pack things. They all whispered talk that I didn't understand. But I had heard that the white people who owned the land were mad. Too many Negroes were leaving and workers were scarce. When people talked openly about leaving, night riders came covered in sheets, burning houses, beating Negroes, stealing their cattle and horses.

Then late one night a neighbor's son came crying for Papa. Night riders had come to their farm. Mama begged Papa not to go. Papa armed all the sons, except me. He told them to protect our house to the death. Then he took his shotgun and rode off with the neighbor.

I shivered with fear. Night riders meant fire and death. We waited. Papa didn't come. We waited and waited. Finally when the light of dawn showed in the east, Papa came home.

He called the family together. I had never seen so much anger and sadness in Papa's face. He said that night riders had learned that our neighbor had returned from Kansas to move his family onto land he had purchased there. Then Papa's voice cracked with emotion when he said night riders had cut off our neighbor's hands and put them in his wife's lap. "Now go to Kansas and work your land with these," they told her. Then Papa cried silent tears.

My brother, Silas, asked Papa if we still had plans to go. Papa said, "We can't stay. Slavery ain't dead here. We must find a place where we can live free."

On hearing this I fell ill with fear and for days burned with fever. I am told that I screamed day and night causing the whole family grave concern. The only thing that made me better was word that the wagon train we were to join had been called off. The families planning to leave were too frightened. They did not tell me, though, that Papa, having made up his mind, was determined to go.

"But we can't go alone," Mama pleaded.

"There are nine of us," Papa answered. "I know the trails like I know the palm of my hand. We will lay in supplies and go."

"Oh, no!" Justin cried aloud. "You had better not try to leave."

"What's going on up there?" Grandpa called to Justin. "I thought you were asleep."

"I'm reading Great-Grandpa's book about coming to Missouri."

"Maybe you had better get down here for some supper."

Justin didn't want to stop reading. He wanted to know if the night riders had come to his great-great-grandpa's farm, too. Did they have trouble leaving Tennessee the way their neighbors had? He also was hungry, ready for supper.

After they had eaten, Grandpa said, "Let's wash the dishes. Would you like to wash or dry?"

Justin was tempted to say "Neither" again. He wanted to get back to the book, but he remembered the guilt he had felt that morning when he had not helped with the dishes. "I'll do them by myself, Grandpa," he said. Then Evelyn's words flashed into his mind: *He'll do nothing but make a mess. . . . We'll be tasting soap for days.* He did not look at Grandpa when he said, "If you'll get me started, I'll do them."

Grandpa showed him how to put in the right amount of water. Justin was sur-prised to learn that on the bottle of the dishwashing liquid it said one capful for dishes. He had been using much, much more than that. Grandpa left him alone.

How nice: no soap spilling over, no splashes on the sink and floor. Soon he had sparkling dishes rinsed and ready for putting away. "I'm done, Grandpa," he said with pride, and raced upstairs to get back to the story of "How We Came to Missouri."

. . . Early the next Saturday morning, I rode with Papa to the market. The ground, hard as stone, was white with frost. The wind blew cold that February morning. I rode on the wagon beside Papa shivering not from the cold, but with fear. Suppose they cut off Papa's hands, I kept thinking. Papa rode quiet with a frown on his brow. I knew he was worried, but not scared.

When we got into town, a lot of Negro men stood together outside the main store. They rushed to crowd around Papa's wagon. They all showed respect and love for Papa. He was prosperous and able to read and write.

We soon learned that the storeowner refused to sell supplies to any Negroes, saying

that without supplies there would be no
more *exodusters*—people leaving going West.
White farmers needed Negroes to work in
menial and some skilled jobs for little pay.
They intended to stop the exodus West.

Papa didn't believe such talk. He walked into the store, cash in hand. Quickly he turned. I didn't believe the look on Papa's face. He did not look as tall, or as strong.

There was no need for talk. That look told everything. I heard the silence on the cold morning air. It was as if every man was holding his breath. Papa climbed into the wagon and flicked the reins. The horses started for home. I heard a neighbor say, "If they refuse to sell to Wiley Ward, we have no hope."

My heart thumped in my chest and a weakness spread over my body down into my legs. I knew now a fear I had never known before. . . .

Justin breathed uneasily, a heaviness in his chest. Suddenly he felt alone, lonely. He longed for home, for Mama, Evelyn, and Hadiya. He closed the book and went in search of his grandpa.

# 9

## ARRIVAL IN MISSOURI

GRANDPA WAS ALREADY in bed, but he was not asleep.

"Can I get in your bed, Grandpa?" Justin asked.

"Sure."

Justin lay close to his grandpa. They did not talk. Finally, Grandpa said, "Do you now know all about 'How We Came to Missouri'?"

"No." There was silence between them again. Then Justin sighed. "It's too sad. I don't want to read anymore."

"But that's about our life, Justin. Why don't you get the book? We'll read it together."

Justin returned with the book and settled comfortably to listen as his grandpa's deep voice read on.

When we got home from the market, Papa told the others what had happened. "We're leaving right away," he said.

"But how can we go by trail without supplies?" my brother Julius asked.

"We will go by boat. Let's take whatever belongings we can. What we can't take, we'll replace at the end of the journey."

Quickly we filled the wagon with the strong packing boxes. We rode all night and part of the next day before coming to the boat landing on the Mississippi River. Hundreds of other Negroes from Alabama, Mississippi, and Georgia lined the shore waiting for passage. Many of them talked of having seen night riders when they tried to vote, own land, or travel freely. They were going West to Canaan Land.

Looking around and listening, I learned that some of those people had nothing at all and some of them didn't know where they were going. They only knew they had to try to get to freedom. Soon after we arrived a shout went up, "Boat's coming!"

I was both excited and upset. We could not get on that boat. Papa first had to sell the horses and wagon. There was no way to take them to Missouri. Suppose that was the last boat for days? People scrambled around us, gathering their belongings. I worried that we'd be alone on the riverfront waiting for the next boat.

"Where're you going?" the captain shouted when the boat finally arrived.

"Kansas," the crowd cried with one voice, ready to scramble aboard.

"We don't haul to Kansas," the captain shouted, and the boat moved on.

Women fell to the ground and cried, "Lord, Lord, what's to come of us?" Some had been there for days. Storekeepers nearby refused to sell them food. Many were without anything to eat and it was bitterly cold.

I got lost from the family. When I found them again Papa, James, and John had gone upriver to try to sell our horses and wagon. The sun glowed red in the west and still they had not returned. Had they been jailed? Would somebody cut off their hands? These thoughts stayed with me even when I went with other boys and men to collect firewood to burn to keep us warm.

Darkness came and I knew I would never see Papa again. . . .

"Did he?" Justin cried. "Tell me, Grandpa. Did he ever see his papa again?"

"We'll have to read on to see," Grandpa said.

. . . We waited. My mother kept quiet and still, but I saw worry in her eyes. We waited and waited. Julius paced up and down, hitting the palm of his hand with the crop of a whip. Still we waited.

Late that night they returned. I ran to them. "Papa, Papa," I cried.

"Leave him be," James said. "Can't you see he's upset?"

John held my hand and said, "We had to give the horses away."

Finally Papa told us that white men refused to buy them. Negroes with money wanted to, but were too scared. Some said they might be accused of helping *exodusters* and be tarred and feathered. Others said they would lose their jobs, go to jail. But worst of all, they would lose the horses and wagon, so why buy them? They must not help anyone leave the South to go West.

Mama broke down and cried.

The next day the wind rose and blew very cold on the river. We huddled close to the fire and drank hot sweet water, and ate cold bread and sorghum.

"What's sorghum, Grandpa?" Justin asked.

"It's a cheap brand of pancake syrup."

"Oh," Justin said, and settled down. "Go on."

. . . The sun seemed far away as we all joined in songs and prayers for our deliverance from this land of trial and tribulation.

As the sun climbed up, almost to the center of the sky, a shout went up, "Boat's coming!"

Papa and three other men pushed forward. They hailed the boat.

"Where y'all wanting to go," a sailor called.

"St. Louis," Papa said in his strong clear voice.

"We can't take niggers into St. Louis and Kansas."

"We veterans of the Civil War," one of the men with Papa shouted. "You can't deny us passage. That's against the law."

"You boys want trouble?" the sailor asked.

"We only want passage," Papa said.

The captain came to the rail. I heard him say to the sailors, "These boys know the law. They could make trouble. We'd better take them on."

We rode up the Mississippi and came to St. Louis. Papa's new-found friends tried to talk him into going on to Kansas. But Papa knew that part of the West well. He knew

that Missouri, unlike Kansas, had been a slave state and that we might have trouble there. But Missouri had many trees from which to build houses. Grass grew tall and green for cattle. Sometimes the wind blew colder than in Tennessee, but not as cold as Kansas.

We found land in the rolling hills of Missouri. Yes, we had troubles. Night riders cut our fences, stole our cattle, and at times burned our hay. But we stayed.

Grandpa turned the open book over and placed it on his chest. Justin sighed and looked up at him, but said nothing.

Finally, Grandpa said, "Yes. We stayed. And we've done well." After a moment of more silence, he said, "Do you know why I asked you to finish the story?"

"I guess you wanted me to know."

"Yes. But more than that, I wanted you to hear it all because you must know where you've come from in order to find the way to where you want to go."

Justin didn't know until the next morning that he had slept all night in Grandpa's bed.

[84]

# 10

## AT LAST, THE FESTIVAL

WHEN JUSTIN AWOKE, Grandpa was already up. Justin jumped from Grandpa's big bed. *The festival starts today,* he thought. Quickly he put on his clothes and joined Grandpa in the kitchen.

Already a fire crackled in the big stove. While Justin put eggs on to boil for breakfast, Grandpa got busy making biscuits from ingredients he had placed on the table the night before. Grandpa planned to enter the Best Biscuit Competition at the festival.

[85]

The rules stated that all biscuits entered must be in the judges' hands by eleven o'clock that morning.

"Can you cook them there?" Justin asked.

"Oh, no. We must cook them at home," Grandpa answered.

"But who will say cold biscuits are good, Grandpa?"

"Why, that's something to think about, son. Hm-m-m. Maybe we should arrive at the festival at five minutes before eleven."

At ten-thirty, Justin and Grandpa raced to the fairgrounds where the festival took place each year. The biscuits, in a heavy hot iron skillet, carefully wrapped in towels to help keep them hot, rested in the back of the truck.

The streets were crowded with people from the town and from neighboring farms. Banners waved all over announcing events. Colorful posters with bucking broncos splashed BILL PICKETT RODEO ads everywhere. People moved up and down streets, car horns honked, friends greeted one an-

[86]

other. Justin wished Anthony was with him for the fun.

Traffic slowed them down. Ten-forty-five: a clock at a savings and loan bank flashed the golden numbers. Justin wondered if they would make it. They were not near the fairgrounds and they had only ten minutes more.

Grandpa kept his eye on the road, driving carefully, and seemingly not a bit worried. But the traffic now moved more slowly than ever.

Soon they reached a stretch of road that led out of town into the country. Grandpa picked up speed. Still Justin worried that they might be late.

Finally the long metal building near the rodeo stands came in view. Its round domelike shape glistened in the late summer sun. Quickly, Grandpa parked the truck and carefully removed the biscuits from the skillet and placed them on a paper plate. He covered them with a gleaming white napkin and rushed inside.

Justin grabbed a lone biscuit left in the

skillet. It was still warm and ever so delicious. While eating it he ran after Grandpa, who was already nearing the far end of the long building. Justin pushed through the crowd after him, hoping Grandpa was not late.

At ten-fifty-nine, Grandpa handed his biscuits to a pleasant-looking lady. She sat behind a table with covered plates of biscuits around her. "You just made it," she said, and smiled at Grandpa.

"I'm glad, too," Grandpa said, returning the lady's smile as he filled out an entry form.

"The judges will announce their decision this evening," the lady said.

"That late?" Justin asked. "They'll be cold, Grandpa."

The lady laughed. "The judging will begin in a minute. It's the decision that will come later."

Justin smiled, relieved. He wished he could get a glimpse of some of the biscuits there under cover. But whose biscuits could taste better than Grandpa's? He knew Grandpa would win.

They moved with the crowd looking at things that had been made by people in the town. All kinds of needlework, quilts, knitted sweaters, scarves, and afghans on display looked inviting. Some had already been judged. Blue, red, and white ribbons announced first, second, and third prizes. Justin wished he could take his mama a beautiful quilt with a big green-and-gold star in the center. But none of those lovely things were for sale.

There were so many things displayed: photography, woodwork. A big model airplane floating from the ceiling surprised Justin. *Wow!* he thought, *that'll get a blue ribbon.*

Soon they came to the display of desserts. Justin had never seen so many scrumptious-looking pies, cakes, brownies, and cookies. He thought of Hadiya and wished she had entered. She'd win for sure.

The pie-eating contest was just about to start. The judges stood ready to determine who could eat the most pie the fastest. Justin stretched up as tall as he could, waving his hand, trying to attract a judge's attention. He knew he could eat a lot of pie. A judge pointed at him. He entered the competition. A whole chocolate pie in front of him did not dim his enthusiasm.

Quickly he ate one piece, two, three, but when he glanced at a boy next to him, he almost choked with surprise. A whole pie had been downed, and all but one piece of another.

If only he hadn't eaten so many biscuits for breakfast, he thought as he finished the last piece on the plate. Another pie was plopped in front of him. But before he could finish the first piece of it, the buzzer sounded. Time up! The boy next to him had eaten all but one piece of his second pie. He won only second place, though. The winner had eaten two whole pies!

"You did good," Justin said to the winner next to him.

The boy sighed, held his stomach, then placed his head on the counter.

"Don," a lady said, putting her hand on his shoulder "You all right?"

"Oh-h-h-h, Ma," Don said.

"We had better move on, Justin," Grandpa said, and led Justin through the crowd.

Justin felt nothing but stuffed. He thought of the boy called Don and was glad the buzzer rang before he had a chance to eat more of that pie. He and Grandpa wandered through the big barnlike building looking at prize-winning carrots, pumpkins, squash, and tomatoes.

Then they decided to go home and feed the animals. Later, they would return for the judges' decisions and the big dance in the pavilion.

Darkness crept over the plains. Justin, ready to go back to the fairgrounds, waited for Grandpa downstairs. He wondered what was keeping him so long. Grandpa had finished showering before him, and Justin had been ready to go for a long time. Justin was anxious to get back. Other contests might be going on.

Finally Grandpa came down the stairs so dressed up that Justin stood surprised.

Never had he seen Grandpa looking so sharp. The suede vest he wore had deep fringe on a yoke in the back and front. His light beige shirt, fitted beige pants, and belt with a big silver buckle were just right with the rich brown vest.

While riding in the truck, Justin sniffed a strange but nice fragrance. Surely Grandpa hadn't put on that smelly stuff Mama forced on him, Justin thought. Now he was glad Anthony was not there. What would he think about Grandpa wearing that stuff? Another whiff came Justin's way. *It's not so bad, though,* he decided. But he liked Grandpa best when he smelled like work, sweet grass, soap—stuff like that.

They arrived just in time for the cake-baking contest. One contestant had entered fifteen cakes—every one a different flavor. Some of them looked too pretty to eat, Justin thought. The judges thought they were perfect. The woman who had baked them won a blue ribbon in every category.

A girl as young as Hadiya won second

place for her lemon chiffon cake. Justin clapped and clapped for her.

Then the judges came to announce the winner for the best biscuits. The lady chosen to do the honors wore a big flower on her bosom and one on her hat. She seemed nervous and dropped all the ribbons. *Why doesn't she hurry up*, Justin thought. His stomach felt weak, his hands were cold. He was now worried that maybe Grandpa would not win.

"First place winner," the lady said in a loud, excited voice, "Phillip Ward, Junior!"

Justin let out a yell. Grandpa smiled and rushed up to get a shiny blue ribbon and a certificate. "The Best Biscuits in the World," the certificate said.

Later at the dance, all the ladies crowded around Grandpa. Many wanted his recipe. Justin stood by holding the blue ribbon and certificate as Grandpa danced, dance after dance with a different partner. He didn't know if the best biscuits or that smelly stuff had wowed all those ladies.

# ♫ 11 ♫

## RODEO TIME

ALREADY THE PARADE was an hour late. Popcorn bags were empty, candy bars all finished, and not a band in sight.

Justin stood with Grandpa right up front. Everyone waited impatiently. Often hand-clapping broke the humdrum and Justin strained to see, but nothing happened.

Finally faraway music alerted the crowd. Soon a marching band led by a lively majorette pranced near enough for Justin to see. Clowns passing out balloons followed the band. With all the color floating around them, the crowd came alive.

Floats representing the months of the year passed slowly. June and November were the most beautiful, Justin thought. June brides with lovely embroidery, fancy quilts, and frilly finery brought cheers. November with gold and brown, Thanksgiving, and bountiful horns of plenty also thrilled the crowd. Others were so much like the exhibit hall that Justin fidgeted, bored. He dared not stop looking, though, in case something interesting came along.

Finally the horses came. Justin cheered and whistled with the crowd. Cowboys from the rodeo in boots and spurs rode tall in their saddles, doffing their cowboy hats. Some did lasso tricks. One cowboy's horse did special dance steps and bowed when the audience applauded.

Then came local cowboys at the very end. Boys and girls rode among them. Justin saw Don who had eaten so much pie. He looked fine on a beautiful sorrel mare.

The crowd followed the parade the short distance to the fairgrounds, where preparations for the games started right away. Every boy and girl was given a list of events. There was so much going on, so much to enter, that Justin didn't know what to do —some twenty events from which to choose four or less. Shearing sheep he knew he could not do. Catching a greased pig, maybe. Spitting watermelon seeds, tossing bean-bags, and pitching horseshoes he might be able to win. He decided to enter four events: spitting watermelon seeds, pitching horseshoes, tossing bean-bags, and kicking his shoe.

While Justin and Grandpa prepared the entry blank Justin saw Don nearby. Justin smiled and waved.

Don came over.

"You from a farm near here?" Don asked.

"My grandpa's ranch, Q–T. But just for the festival," Justin answered.

"Which ones did you enter?" Don asked.

Justin told him the four events.

"All of those are easy. I'm going for sack racing, sheep shearing, and the greased pig," Don said proudly.

Justin, surprised that a boy who looked

no older and bigger than he knew so much, asked, "Where you from?"

"Not far from here. We own sheep and I've come to the festival every year since I was a baby."

"How long is that?" Justin asked.

"Twelve years." Don talked a lot. Justin listened because he had never spit watermelon seeds or kicked his shoe off. Because he played basketball, he felt he might do well pitching horseshoes and tossing bean-bags.

"Try catching the greased pig with me," Don said.

"I don't know about that," Justin said, and looked at Grandpa.

"It's easy," Don said.

Grandpa laughed. "I wouldn't say it's easy, but it's fun. Try it if you want to."

"What event can I take off?" Justin asked.

Grandpa and Don looked over the list with Justin. "Maybe spitting seeds," Justin said.

"Pitching horseshoes, I'd think," Don said. "That's tougher than spitting seeds."

Justin didn't want Don to think that he

could do only easy things, so he entered greased pig instead of spitting seeds.

After Justin and Grandpa had cheered when Don sheared his sheep faster than anyone, it was time for Justin to kick his shoe. He lined up with boys big and small, short and tall. They untied their right shoes and loosed the strings.

"The winner is the one who kicks his shoe the farthest distance," the referee said. "OK, get ready. Kick!"

Justin stepped forward on his left foot and kicked so that his shoe flew off his foot, up and out. The crowd cheered as shoes sailed away. They laughed and scrambled out of the way as some shoes went straight up and fell very close by.

Justin watched his shoe soar away, but not far enough. When they measured he learned he had won third place. He was happy.

The sack race proved fun to watch. Boys and girls hopped along. Those who tried to run stumbled, toppled over, and rolled. Justin rocked with laughter. Don fell so many times, he didn't even place.

[99]

Justin's basketball skills paid off. He easily won first prize tossing the bean-bag through the holes in a big board, and tied for second in pitching horseshoes.

Then it was time to catch the greased pig. The little pig, round and fat, waited in a crate about three feet away from the boys and girls ready to chase and catch it. The crate sprang open and the pig ran toward them. Justin raced ahead. The pig moved right in reach. He grabbed, but it slipped through his hands. *Like trying to catch an eel*, Justin thought. Every time Justin knew he had the pig—swish—it was gone. He was stumbling and falling, still hoping to grab it and hang on. No one had any better luck.

One time Justin thought Don might get hold, but the pig scrambled wildly away from the chase. Then finally a girl dashed for the pig and fell down with one of the pig's feet caught under her chest. She hugged him to her and became the winner.

Justin, hot, sweaty, and dusty, had never

had so much fun. He counted his ribbons: one white, third place; one red, second place; and one first place, blue. He knew Grandpa was proud of him, but he wondered, *What will Evelyn say when she sees these?*

Justin walked through the crowds at the fairgrounds with Grandpa, his chest swelling with happiness. Now he would see the cowboys he had heard so much about in action.

Grandpa guided him through the surging crowd. A tall cowboy hat and high-heeled boots made his slim grandpa look even taller. With a feeling of pride, Justin hitched up his jeans, glad he had brought his cowboy belt with the silver buckle. He wished he had a cowboy hat.

The smells of barbecue, baked beans, and popcorn tempted the crowd. Grandpa ordered barbecued ribs for Justin and a hot link sandwich for himself while Justin ordered tall cold drinks for them both.

All over the arena colorful banners

splashed: BILL PICKETT COWBOY RODEO SHOW. Justin whispered, "Grandpa, is there another Bill Pickett?"

Grandpa smiled, "Oh, no. Cowboys today, knowing what a good showman William Pickett was, name their show after him."

Cowboy music got the crowd in a mood for action. First cowboys on lively horses galloped around the arena. Then two clowns ran in. One was a lady dressed in a long skirt and pantalettes. Suddenly a voice over a speaker said, "Howdy, partners. Welcome! The famous Bill Pickett Rodeo is about to get under way. Cowboys and cowgirls will ride, rope, and bulldog. You ready, partners?"

The crowd roared, "Ready!"

Suddenly a bull shot out of a gate like a silver bullet, a cowboy on his back. At first Justin was so scared he couldn't look. The crowd roared its satisfaction. Justin finally peeked through his fingers. The cowboy was still riding. The bull was bucking, pitching, rocking, and rolling. The rider still stayed on, squeezing, hugging,

[102]

and holding that bull with his legs. Then the bull moved like it was waltzing, and the rider fell to the ground.

Instantly the bull turned and plunged at the rider. Justin screamed, "Watch out!" The clowns rushed in, waving banners of cloth to distract the bull. The bull ran away into the corral.

The next event was the lady clown riding a bull. She seemed hardly able to hang on. The bull tossed her about. Her hat and wig came off. Then her dress came off and Justin knew that it was no lady at all. Everybody laughed.

"Ladies and gentlemen," the voice over the speaker called. "Give the rider a hand. That's Rooster. He's not a clown, but one of our best 'pickup men.' Let's hear it for Rooster, partners."

"What are 'pickup men,' Grandpa?" Justin asked.

"They're men who rescue fallen cowboys, or pick them off horses so they won't get trampled."

The cheering was interrupted. "Now, partners, we have the best broncobuster

[103]

since Jessie Stahl, who rode Glasseye. Watch this cowboy from Laredo, Texas," the announcer said. "He will ride a bronco that's as hot as cayenne pepper and as explosive as a volcano."

"Think he'll be as good as Jessie Stahl, Grandpa?" Justin asked.

Before his grandpa answered, the rider came out on a bucking horse between Rooster and another pickup man. The horse streaked into the arena jumping, spinning, and shaking. With its head down it bucked high in the air. The rider stayed on. The horse pitched, plunged, jumped high, twisting in midair. Still the rider stayed without holding on to the saddle horn.

"Why doesn't he hold on to the saddle, Grandpa?" Justin asked.

"If he touches the saddle horn, he will be disqualified and cannot win a prize."

The crowd, up on its feet, roared while that horse tried to toss the rider. The horse started to run and the pickup men rushed in and pulled the rider off its back. The rider had won.

The horse ran all over the arena snorting and kicking as the crowd still stood, roaring.

Justin wondered what would happen if that horse jumped over into the stands.

"That rider is good," Grandpa said. "He's

young, too. He might outbest Jessie one day, but he isn't there yet."

Then the cowgirls' turn came. Women in pretty costumes rode fast-moving horses around barrels. The crowd watched to see which rider could race around four barrels then back to the field in the shortest time. Justin's heart seemed to stand still as one rider, moving as fast as the wind, rode very close to the barrels. He felt sure she would run into a barrel and fall off her horse. But she didn't touch a single barrel and became the winner. Justin shouted with joy.

When the crowd settled, the announcer was telling about calf roping and of another famous Black cowboy, Nate Love. Justin remembered Nate Love, nicknamed Deadwood Dick. He looked at Grandpa and smiled as the announcer went on, "Not only did Nate rope and tie calves, he roped and tied wild mustangs, too. Today, let's watch a young cowboy from Prairie View, Texas, rope and tie calves."

Justin jumped to his feet as a black calf came out of one gate and a cowboy on a horse came out of another. The race was on. Finally the cowboy threw his lasso and stopped the calf. The cowboy slid off his horse, threw the calf to the ground, folded its legs, and tied three of them together. Then he raised his hands to let the judges know he was done. The horse moved slowly backward, tightening the rope just enough to keep the calf in place.

Would the calf stay tied six seconds so the cowboy could win? Justin waited. The calf did not wriggle loose. Justin roared with the crowd. "What will his prize be?" Justin asked.

"Money," Grandpa answered.

At last the event Justin had been waiting for arrived. The bulldogging began. A big black steer with long sharp horns raced out of a gate. Two cowboys on horses shot out after it. Suddenly, one of the cowboys jumped off his horse and grabbed the steer's horns. He wrestled the steer to the ground, twisting its head back until its nose was up. This was done so quickly and easily that Justin stood and cheered with the crowd.

"That's the way Bill Pickett did it, eh, Grandpa?"

"Yes, but even faster and easier," Grandpa said.

When Justin was sadly thinking all the fun was over, the voice boomed over the loudspeaker. "All boys and girls ten years and younger can now become cowboys and cowgirls. We are going to let loose some baby Brahman bulls. Three of them will have red ribbons on their tails. The boy or girl who gets a ribbon will win a prize."

Justin listened and wondered if he should try. *A cowboy needs a hat,* he thought. *If only I had a cowboy hat.* Suddenly he said to himself, *If I win prize money, I will buy a hat.* "Grandpa," he asked, "can I try?"

"Sure you can. And bring back a ribbon, you hear?"

Justin waited at the gate with the other boys and girls who also wanted to try. The sharp horsy smell floated over him. He felt good and at ease with that smell he loved so much.

The gate to let the baby Brahmans out

opened at the same time as the gate to let the boys and girls onto the field. The scramble was on as the blue-gray Brahmans raced about.

Justin waited. Then he saw a baby bull that he could head off and chase in the opposite direction.

The bull calf stopped and faced Justin. Justin stopped, too. He put his hands on his hips and looked at the bull. Suddenly Justin had an idea. He would grab that bull and wrestle it to the ground and draw cheers from the crowd the way the other cowboys had done.

Justin moved forward. *Oh, no,* he thought. *This bull has no horns! A dogie needs horns.* As he looked the bull in the eye it turned and ran away, waving its tail.

A red ribbon fluttered. In the nick of time, Justin snatched it. A winner!

When the judge awarded the prizes, he placed a cowboy hat on Justin's head. The crowd roared. Justin waved the red ribbon and though he knew he could not be heard over the cheers, he shouted anyway. "I'm a real cowboy now, Grandpa!"

[109]

# 12

## JUSTIN'S TRIUMPH

THE END OF the festival marked the end of the visit. The day for Justin to go home had arrived. *Good times go fast*, he thought as he packed his things, feeling both happy and sad. Happy because he had enjoyed himself and was going home; sad because he had to leave Grandpa.

He had so much to tell his family and his friend Anthony. He could hardly wait to tell Anthony about Don and the pies. Then he thought of Evelyn. *How surprised she'll be when she sees the ribbons and the hat.*

[110]

*Wait'll she sees that I can make a bed smooth as glass and wash dishes sparkly clean,* he thought, and smiled. Then he remembered the burning rice. *If only I could show her I can cook, too.*

Suddenly Justin had an idea. Hurriedly he finished packing and went to Grandpa's room. Grandpa was just getting dressed.

"I guess you're anxious to leave me," Grandpa said. "You're up so early."

"Oh, no. I don't want to leave you." He hugged Grandpa around the waist.

"We had fun, eh?"

"Best time I ever had. Grandpa, can you show me how to make your biscuits?"

"Think you can learn how to make the best biscuits in the world?"

"I want to try."

"All right. The first thing we'll do is wash our hands carefully."

After they had washed their hands, Grandpa said, "Now we'll need to make some dishwater."

"Why dishwater, Grandpa?" Justin asked.

[111]

"A good cook always cleans as he goes along. Then the place is not a mess when everything is cooked."

Grandpa showed Justin how he made biscuit mix with flour, powdered milk, baking powder, and salt. *So that's why he only added shortening and water when he made his biscuits*, Justin thought.

Grandpa let Justin measure the shortening and the right amount of water. "Remember now," Grandpa said, "the secret of good biscuits is in your touch. Handle the dough with tender loving care."

The bigger part of the morning went by with them in the kitchen. Justin learned to measure, mix, and bake biscuits. He learned how to cook stewed raisins and smoked pork, too.

Now, feeling he knew how to cook, Justin raced out to the meadow to say goodbye to the horses and to share with them some leftover biscuits. He stood for a moment looking at the blackish-green rolling hills in the distance. No fog floated like clouds today. The sky, crystal clear, was as blue as the lake.

[112]

He gave Cropper a biscuit first; he petted Palaver, gave him a biscuit, walked away, and whistled. Black came on the run. Justin pulled his head down. Hugging Black's head, Justin rubbed Black's velvety nose with his own. He let Black nibble the gift slowly. "Goodbye, boy. Be good, now. See you soon." Slowly he walked back to the house, wishing he didn't have to leave.

By the time all the chores were done, animals fed and watered, the afternoon had moved toward early evening.

Finally the Iron Pony, packed with eggs, ham, Justin's biscuit mix, raisins, and pork, was ready to go. The bag of goodies had written on it: *For Justin's hands and eyes only. Do not look, do not touch.*

On the road, Justin's excitement doubled. He could hardly wait to see them all back home. Even though Grandpa stopped only once for gas, they arrived way after dark. Already the family was in bed. Mama let them in, delighted to have them home.

"We had better say our goodbye now," Grandpa said to Justin. "By the time you get up in the morning, I'll be well on the way back to the ranch."

Grandpa stooped for Justin's hug and kiss. " 'Bye, Grandpa. Thanks for the best time ever," Justin said.

Even though he was very tired and sleepy, Justin noticed that nothing had changed in his room. He got into his lumpy bed knowing that a lot of work lay ahead of him. He fell asleep, happy to be home.

The next morning he slept late. It was almost noon when the sound of the telephone woke him. *What is that?* he wondered, then remembered he was home. He jumped out of bed, rummaged through his desk, and found a big white card. PLEASE DO NOT DISTURB, he wrote. Then he punched in two holes. Using one of his old shoelaces, he hung the card on the doorknob, and set to work.

First he pulled everything out of the closet. He replaced his shirts, hanging them so they did not touch. Then his jackets. Finally the closet looked neat. He stood back and smiled. *I did that all by myself.*

Now the bed. After he had removed the

sheets and the light blanket, he carefully put them on again the way Grandpa had shown him. At first, he forgot what Grandpa had said. How should he tuck the blanket and sheets at the foot of the bed in angles? He tried to see it in his mind. Triangle! It was easy now. His bed looked almost as smooth as Hadiya's.

He had to do something to his walls, he thought. But he couldn't decide whether to remove a football, basketball, or rock star. Where would he put his ribbons? And his hat? There was no space. What could he do?

Suddenly he got the idea to count backward from ten. The picture his hand touched when he reached zero would have to go. Wow! Just missed his favorite, Halley's Comet. He was glad that the one on zero was not one he really cared about. He was happy, too, that the space was big enough for his hat and ribbons.

"Justin, Justin," Evelyn called, and knocked on his door.

He locked the door and answered, "Yeah?"

[115]

"Don't you want to see us?"

Quickly he unlocked the door and stepped outside. "You mean you want to see me?"

"Sure, stupid," Evelyn said, hugging him. Hadiya stood by, smiling.

Justin hugged them both, feeling good inside.

"What's this 'Do Not Disturb' and that bag in the fridge, 'don't look, don't touch'?" Hadiya asked. "I'm coming in."

Justin blocked the door. "No way, and you'd better not bother my bag."

"How would you know if I did?" Hadiya asked.

"I'll know, and if you don't believe me, try it."

"Aw, Justin, let us see."

"No." He went into his room and quickly closed his door.

"You think you're so great since you've been with Grandpa," Evelyn shouted through the closed door.

Justin stayed in his room, pleased that he had them guessing. He wished there was a way to get them out of the house. With them away, he'd feel more at ease trying to cook a surprise supper for the family.

Now knowing that Hadiya and Evelyn liked him and wanted him back, he thought about going to the playground. But he still had work to do.

The phone rang. Again Evelyn knocked on his door. "Justin, Mama called. She's coming home early. Hadiya and I are going to the mall. Want to come?"

His heart pounded with excitement. *They'll be out of the house! No way will I go,* he thought. He didn't like shopping with them anyway. They took forever. He begged off.

When Mama came home, Justin rushed to meet her. "Can I cook supper for us?"

"Justin, no."

"But, why, Mama?"

"I don't want you messing in my kitchen."

He tried to assure her that he could cook without being messy. *A good cook always*

*starts with clean hands and clean dishwater.*
*Clean up as you go along.* Grandpa's words
and example guided his plea.

"Please, Mama. I know what to do," he
begged.

"But I don't want you in the kitchen."

"I can do it. Just try me. And promise
you won't come in unless I call you, OK?"

"OK."

Now that he had the go-ahead, he felt
frightened. Would he remember all he had
done when Grandpa showed him how to
make biscuits: just enough shortening, not
too much water? He placed the bag with
all of his ingredients on the counter.

More worried about the biscuits than
about the raisins and pork, he decided to
make biscuits first. After putting the mix
in a bowl he made a round hole in the
center of the mix just as Grandpa had.
Then he added shortening, mixed it in,
and added water. He tried to blend it all
together with his fingers. It felt too icky,
he thought. He used a spoon to work in
more mix with tender loving care.

When he began to think it was taking

[118]

longer than he remembered, his mama called at the door, "Justin, you all right in there?"

Maybe he should ask her. But he called, "I'm OK," hoping the dough would become smooth and round.

Finally he had twelve biscuits, close together, on a greased shiny pan.

The biscuits safe on the counter, he quickly washed the bowl and spoon. Now he was ready for the next task. The pork. It took the longest to cook. He found a heavy skillet and put the pork in it with a little water. With the fire turned low, he waited and watched. He didn't want it to burn. Pretty soon it boiled slowly. He smiled and put the raisins in a pot to prepare them the way Grandpa had shown him. Turning the fire very low under them, he noticed that the pork was now bubbling in its own fat.

Mama called again, "Need me, Justin?"

"Not yet."

"OK. It smells like you know what you're doing."

Finally, he went to find Mama to tell her

[119]

he was ready to turn on the oven. She wanted to come into the kitchen even though she knew he had turned the oven on before.

"No, no, not yet. I can do it," he pleaded.

The biscuits went into a hot 425-degree oven. Justin was very careful. With the oven door closed, he called Mama to set the timer for fifteen minutes. "Now come in, but don't open the oven, and don't look in the pots!"

Before the biscuits were done, he heard Hadiya and Evelyn come back from shopping.

"Mama," Hadiya called. "What's smelling so good? I'm starved."

He heard Mama say, "That's Justin cooking, and don't go in the kitchen."

The buzzer sounded. The biscuits were done. He opened the oven door and was surprised to see golden biscuits. *It is magic,* he thought.

The raisins stewed, plump in their juice; the pork bubbled, brown and crisp. He called to Mama, "You can help me now."

She helped put the food on the table.

[120]

Evelyn and Hadiya were invited to share Justin's supper. They all took generous helpings.

Hadiya bit into a biscuit. "*M-mm-m*, Justin, these are the best biscuits in the world."

"Who believes Justin did these delicious biscuits?" Evelyn asked.

"I do, because he did," Mama answered with great pride.

Justin beamed with pleasure.

Later, he invited them all to his room for open house to see the prize ribbons and hat he had won at the festival.

"Can you believe this room?" Evelyn cried as she entered. "Look at his bed, wow!"

Mama smiled. "I'll give you first prize for your room," she said, hugging him.

"And I'll give you a gold medal for the best biscuits in the world," Hadiya said.

"How'd you ever do it?" Evelyn wanted to know.

Justin felt he would burst with happiness. "Aw, it's easy when you know how," he said matter-of-factly. When he winked like Grandpa, they all laughed.